Matt Driv

by Mi

Pioneer Valley Educational Press, Inc.

Matt said, "Dad,
can we go to the mall?"

"OK," said Dad.

"Can I drive?" said Matt.

"Yes," said Dad.
"Here is the key."

"Matt, you are going
too fast," said Dad.

"Oh, Dad," said Matt.
"I'm not going too fast!"

"Slow down!"
said Dad.

"Look out, Matt," said Dad. "A car is coming!"

"Yes, Dad. I can see the car," said Matt.

"Look out, Matt!" said Dad.
"A truck is coming!"

"Yes, Dad," said Matt.
"I can see the truck."

"Oh, good," said Dad.

"Oh no!" said Dad.
"Here comes a bike!"

"I can see the bike,"
said Matt.

"Oh, good!" said Dad.

"Oh no, Matt," said Dad. "You have stopped the car."

"Look, Dad," said Matt.
"We are at the mall."

"Oh, good," said Dad.
"We are at the mall,
and we are **safe**!"